This igloo book belongs to:

....

igloobooks

Published in 2013
by Igloo Books Ltd
Cottage Farm
Sywell
NN6 0BJ
www.igloobooks.com

FIR003 1113
2 4 6 8 10 9 7 5 3 1
ISBN 978-1-78197-147-5

Printed and manufactured in China

Illustrated by Natalie Hinrichsen, Marina Le Ray and James Newman Gray

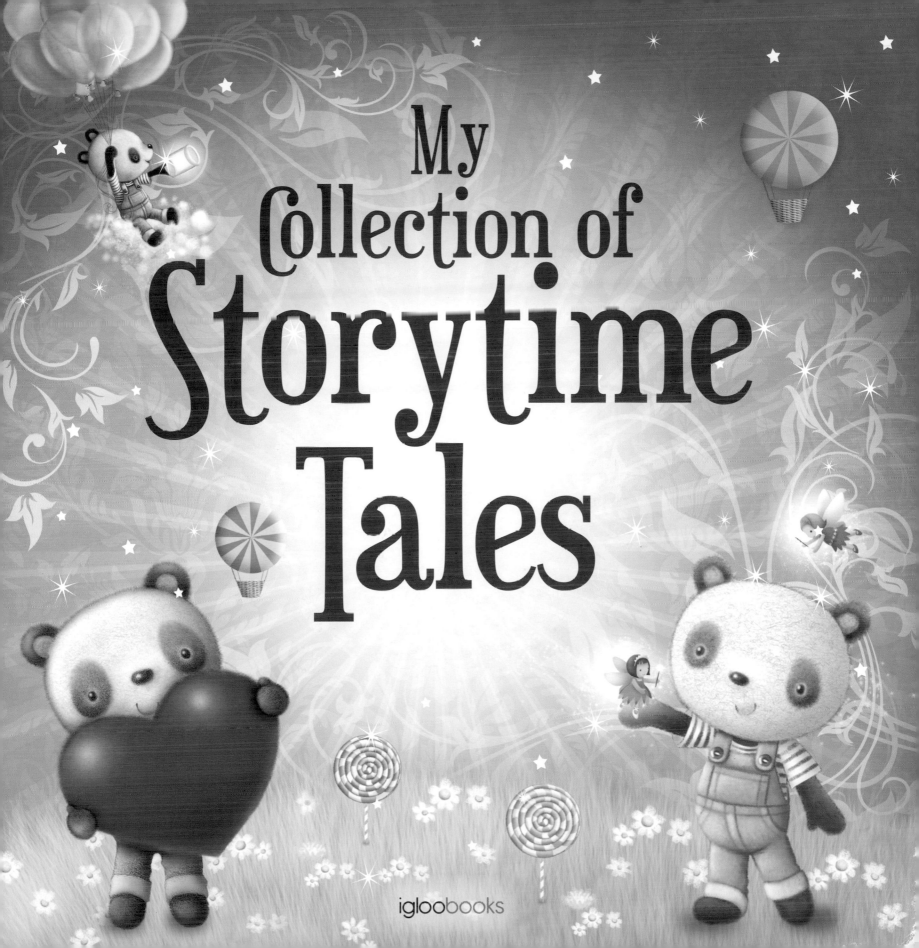

My Collection of Storytime Tales

igloobooks

Contents

Old MacDonald had a Farm

Old MacDonald had a farm, E-I-E-I-O,
and on that farm he had some hens, E-I-E-I-O.

With a cluck-cluck here and a cluck-cluck there,
here a cluck, there a cluck, everywhere a cluck-cluck.
Old MacDonald had a farm, E-I-E-I-O.

Old MacDonald had a farm, E-I-E-I-O,
and on that farm he had some chicks, E-I-E-I-O.

With a cheep-cheep here and a cheep-cheep there,
here a cheep, there a cheep, everywhere a cheep-cheep.
Old MacDonald had a farm, E-I-E-I-O.

Old MacDonald had a farm, E-I-E-I-O,
and on that farm he had some cows, E-I-E-I-O.

With a moo-moo here and a moo-moo there,
here a moo, there a moo, everywhere a moo-moo.
Old MacDonald had a farm, E-I-E-I-O.

Old MacDonald had a farm, E-I-E-I-O,
and on that farm he had a horse, E-I-E-I-O.

With a neigh-neigh here and a neigh-neigh there,
here a neigh, there a neigh, everywhere a neigh-neigh.
Old MacDonald had a farm, E-I-E-I-O.

Old MacDonald had a farm, E-I-E-I-O,
and on that farm he had some pigs, E-I-E-I-O.

With an oink-oink here and an oink-oink there,
here an oink, there an oink, everywhere an oink-oink.
Old MacDonald had a farm, E-I-E-I-O.

Old MacDonald had a farm, E-I-E-I-O,
and on that farm he had some ducks, E-I-E-I-O.

With a quack-quack here and a quack-quack there,
here a quack, there a quack, everywhere a quack-quack.
Old MacDonald had a farm, E-I-E-I-O.

Old MacDonald had a farm, E-I-E-I-O,
and on that farm he had a dog, E-I-E-I-O.

With a woof-woof here and a woof-woof there,
here a woof, there a woof, everywhere a woof-woof.
Old MacDonald had a farm, E-I-E-I-O.

Old MacDonald had a farm, E-I-E-I-O,
and on that farm he had some sheep, E-I-E-I-O.

With a baa-baa here and a baa-baa there,
here a baa, there a baa, everywhere a baa-baa.
Old MacDonald had a farm, E-I-E-I-O.

Old MacDonald had a farm, E-I-E-I-O,
and on that farm he had some mice, E-I-E-I-O.

With a squeak-squeak here and a squeak-squeak there,
here a squeak, there a squeak, everywhere a squeak-squeak.
Old MacDonald had a farm, E-I-E-I-O.

Old MacDonald had a farm, E-I-E-I-O,
and on that farm he had a cat, E-I-E-I-O.

With a miaow-miaow here and a miaow-miaow there,
here a miaow, there a miaow, everywhere a miaow-miaow.
Old MacDonald had a farm, E-I-E-I-O.

Old MacDonald had a farm, E-I-E-I-O,
and on that farm he had some animals, E-I-E-I-O.

With a cluck, cheep, neigh and a moo, oink, quack,
here a woof, there a baa, everywhere a miaow, squeak!
Old MacDonald had a farm, E-I-E-I-O.

The Wheels on the Bus

The wheels on the bus go round and round,
round and round, round and round.
The wheels on the bus go round and round, all through the town.

The animals on the bus get on and off,
on and off, on and off.
The animals on the bus get on and off, all through the town.

The money on the bus goes jingle, jangle, jingle, jingle, jangle, jingle, jingle, jangle, jingle.
The money on the bus goes jingle, jangle, jingle, all through the town.

The driver on the bus goes, "Move on back,
move on back, move on back."
The driver on the bus goes, "Move on back," all through the town.

The motor on the bus goes vroom, vroom, vroom,
vroom, vroom, vroom, vroom, vroom, vroom.
The motor on the bus goes vroom, vroom, vroom, all through the town.

The horn on the bus goes beep, beep, beep,
beep, beep, beep, beep, beep, beep.
The horn on the bus goes beep, beep, beep, all through the town.

The mother hippos go chatter, chatter, chatter,
chatter, chatter, chatter, chatter, chatter, chatter.
The mother hippos go chatter, chatter, chatter, all through the town.

The daddy elephants go nod, nod, nod,
nod, nod, nod, nod, nod, nod.
The daddy elephants go nod, nod, nod, all through the town.

The wipers on the bus go swish, swish, swish,
swish, swish, swish, swish, swish, swish.
The wipers on the bus go swish, swish, swish, all through the town.

The puddles on the road go splash, splash, splash,
splash, splash, splash, splash, splash, splash.
The puddles on the road go splash, splash, splash, all through the town.

The baby lion cubs go, "Wah, wah, wah,
wah, wah, wah, wah, wah, wah."
The baby lion cubs go, "Wah, wah, wah,"all through the town.

The little tiger tots go giggle, giggle, giggle,
giggle, giggle, giggle, giggle, giggle, giggle.
The little tiger tots go giggle, giggle, giggle, all through the town.

The traffic lights outside go stop, wait, go,
stop, wait, go, stop, wait, go.
The traffic lights outside go stop, wait, go, all through the town.

The signals on the bus go blink, blink, blink,
blink, blink, blink, blink, blink, blink.
The signals on the bus go blink, blink, blink, all through the town.

ABC

The grandpa gorillas go snore, snore, snore,
snore, snore, snore, snore, snore, snore.
The grandpa gorillas go snore, snore, snore, all through the town.

The grandma crocodiles go shh, shh, shh,
shh, shh, shh, shh, shh, shh.
The grandma crocodiles go shh, shh, shh, all through the town.

The bus goes round town until the sun goes down,
the sun goes down, the sun goes down.
The bus goes round town until the sun goes down, all through the town.

The animals on the bus go, "Here's my stop!
Here's my stop! Here's my stop!"
The animals on the bus go, "Here's my stop!"...

... all through the town.

When the weather is cloudy, if there's just one thing I could do,
It would be to float up in the sky and bring sunshine home to you.

I'd catch the golden rays in a jar that glows bright and warm,
To keep you nice and cosy when there's a scary storm.

To show you how much I love you,
I'd make you a special treat.
It would be the yummiest cake ever,
just for you to eat.

My cake would be big and tall and
covered in lovely, pink cream.
It would be a yummy, scrummy,
sticky, candy-licking dream.

57

I would do anything to cheer you up when you're feeling down.
I'd put on a funny show for you and dress up as a clown.

I'd get my friends to dress up in a silly, circus style,
Then I'd wobble on a tightrope, just to try and make you smile.

In a magic wood, I'd find out
where the fairies go to hide.
I'd make a wish in the fairy
ring and dance around inside.

Fairies would come with their wands
and flutter here and there.
I would make a wish for you to
show you how much I care.

61

I'd turn into a superhero and become Super Panda Bear.
If you needed me, I'd zoom up high and fly through the air.

I'd whoosh over the city, across the mountains and the sea.
When I finally reach you, you'd get a super-hug from me.

I love you so much, I would gather clouds to make a lovely bed,
With the warmest fluffy blanket and a pillow for your head.

I'd imagine you were with me and ready for a rest,
Then I'd read you all the stories that I know you'd like the best.

To show you how much I love you,
I'd climb a ladder to the sky.
It would reach past clouds and
sunbeams and rainbows way up high.

My ladder would stretch up to the
stars and they would shine so bright.
I'd bring the biggest one back for you,
to twinkle through the night.

I'd go up to the mountain top and shout so everyone could hear. Then I'd run back down to whisper, "I love you," in your ear.

I want to tell the world just how special you are to me,
And that when I'm with you, I'm as happy as can be.

I love you so much because I think that you're the very best.
You're all warm and cuddly and much snugglier than the rest.

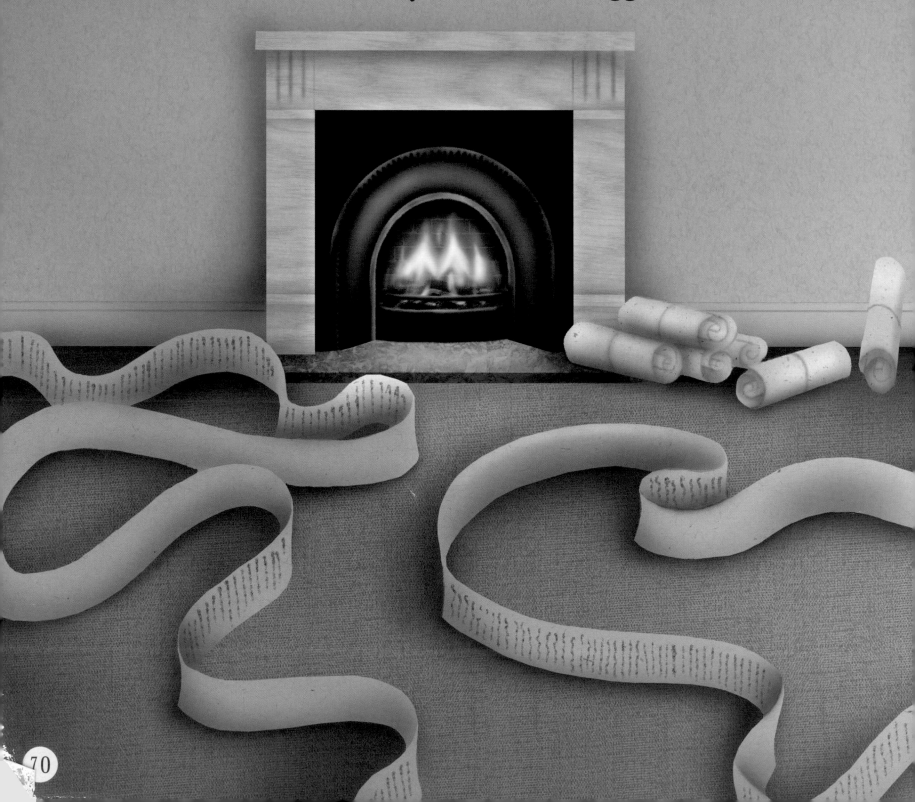

I can think of lots of ways to tell you how lovely you are,
To let you know what you mean to me and that you're my shining star.

I'm so lucky that I have you and you'll always have me, too.
I love you more than anyone, just because you're you!